The Knot in the Tracks

by ROBERTO PIUMINI • pictures by MIKHAIL FEDOROV

Translated from the Italian by Olivia Holmes

TAMBOURINE BOOKS NEW YORK

LIBRARY OF CONGRESS CATALOGING IN PUBLICATION DATA

Piumini, Roberto. [Pastrisciuz e il diavolo racso. English] The knot in the tracks/by Roberto Piumini; pictures by Mikhail Nikolayevich Fedorov; translated from

the Italian by Olivia Holmes. — 1st ed. p. cm. Summary: In faraway Siberia, along the tracks for the Trans-Siberian Railroad, a railroad worker is plagued by a

bullying demon who insists on tying the tracks in knots. ISBN 0-688-11166-1. — ISBN 0-688-11167-X (lib. bdg.) [1. Demonology—Fiction. 2. Trans-Siberian

Railway—Fiction. 3. Railroads—Fiction. 4. Siberia (Russia)—Fiction.] I. Fedorov, Mikhail Nikolayevich, ill. II. Title. PZ7.P6894Kn 1994 [e]—dc20 93-20343 CIP AC

1 3 5 7 9 10 8 6 4 2

First edition

In faraway Siberia runs the Trans-Siberian Railroad—two rails stretching across the silent and deserted plain from horizon to horizon. The train used to pass just once a week.

A railroad worker named Petrushka lived by himself in a house beside the tracks. The only people he ever saw were the passengers on the train that sped by every Tuesday, and they never even noticed him.

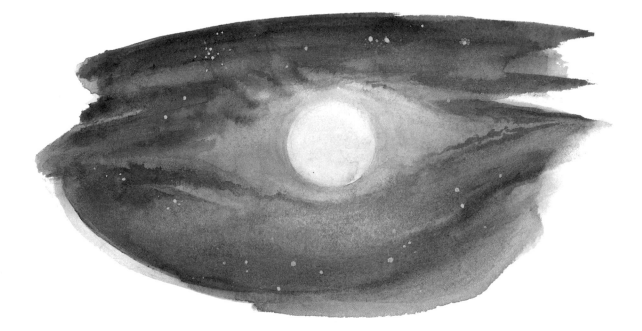

But he was happy with his lot, and spent most of his time walking along the tracks, making sure that the railway was always in good repair.

One Tuesday evening, a few hours after the passage of the eastbound train, Petrushka went out with his lamp for a last look at the tracks. An icy wind was blowing, and he wanted to get back quickly to his warm stove and the cabbage soup cooking on it. But Petrushka had his job to do, so he walked eastward along the iron rails.

After about a hundred yards he thought he saw a strange flickering light. He walked faster. Then he stopped short with his mouth hanging open while his lamp wavered in the wind.

The two rails were knotted together like big steel strings.

"Ha, ha, ha, that's a funny joke, isn't it, Brother Petrushka?" said a nasty little voice in the darkness.

The startled trackwalker lifted his lamp. The light fell on a dark, ugly little man with huge, hairy ears and hands bigger than his whole face. He was sitting cross-legged on a rotten old fur rug.

"Who are you, and what have you done?" gasped Petrushka.

"Why ask questions when you can see for yourself?" sneered the little man, the wind splaying his hairy ears. "My name is Rashka, and I'm a demon. I may not be much of a demon, but still I've made a nice knot in your rails!"

"The rails aren't mine!" wailed Petrushka. "They belong to the railroad, and the train has to pass through here. You can't leave them like this, or the train will crash!"

Rashka made funny grimaces of surprise. "Why, what do you know! Who would ever have thought it?"

"Please, Rashka," implored Petrushka, "undo the knot."

"Make me some tea first," said the demon, jumping to his feet. "Make me a good hot tea of orange and mint leaves. Then we will see about this little knot."

"But orange and mint leaves only grow beyond the mountains in the south. It takes three days to walk there!"

"Hup to it, then! I'll wait right here for the tea you've promised me."

Petrushka begged and pleaded, but the ugly little monster made no reply. He just lay down on the smelly fur like a dead wolf and went to sleep.

With a knot in his chest, the trackwalker ran home. He filled his knapsack and canteen. Then he loaded his lamp with oil and headed south into the wind. When he fell down exhausted at dawn, he could just barely see the mountains in the distance. He ate a few crackers and berries, slept for a while, then began walking again.

At the end of the second day he reached the mountains and started climbing. At the end of the third, he saw a flowered plain below him and rushed downhill like a waterfall.

He ran around madly, picking mint leaves and orange blossoms. Then he started back, sleeping only when he couldn't go on any longer.

He arrived home late Monday night. He put a pot of water on the stove, let it boil, and threw the leaves and blossoms in. He strained it, then ran along the rails to the knot.

The world paled with the light of dawn.

Rashka was seated on his rug with a dirty tin cup in his hand.

Petrushka poured the tea into it.

"Nice and hot, the way I like it," said Rashka, wiping his mouth on the filthy fur. "And now let's see about this knot."

While Petrushka watched, trembling with cold and exhaustion, the demon stood up and passed his big hands over the rails. They loosened like eels and became hard and straight again.

Without a word the demon left, but Petrushka didn't budge. He wanted to see the passing of the westbound train.

After about two hours the train did puff along by in the broadening daylight. Not one of the passengers drowsing in the coaches even noticed Petrushka kneeling in the grass.

The trackwalker slept for two whole days after that. Then he ate bowl after bowl of cabbage soup and once more took up his life beside the rails.

But one month later Petrushka found the tracks knotted again.

Rashka was sitting beside them scratching his belly. "What do you want now, Demon Rashka? Why have you made another knot?"

"You have to realize, Brother Petrushka, that it's easy for demons to do wicked things like this, but much harder for us to do harmless things like looking for tea leaves, for example — or finding red pebbles to make necklaces."

"So?" asked Petrushka, with an aching heart.

"So . . . so . . . my brother," said Rashka, rocking back and forth, "so this knot has got to be untied before the next train passes. I just saw one go by, speeding like the blazes. But the next? Bring me a hundred red pebbles from the mountains in the north, the little stones that are good for making necklaces, and I'll untie the knot."

"But those mountains are four days' walk from here. How can I go and come back in a week?"

"The wind goes and comes back again all in one morning, brother, and the birds in an afternoon. Is a man less than they are? Do what I say: Bring me one hundred red pebbles, or this knot will not be loosened!"

Petrushka fell on his knees in desperation, while his eyes searched the dark for distant mountains. But a moment later he jumped to his feet and ran back home to prepare his lamp and knapsack.

He hiked northward in the night until he could go no further. Then he rested a bit and went on. He reached the mountains in just two and a half days, found a hundred pebbles in one day, and made it home in three more days.

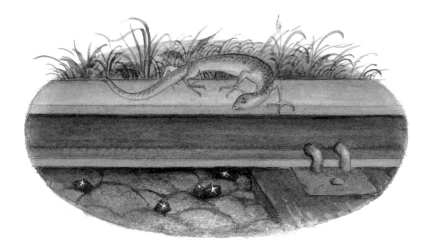

It was less than an hour until the eastbound train was due to pass. He counted the pebbles from his knapsack and put them in a little bag. Then he set off toward the knot, walking in the middle of the tracks.

"Welcome back from your stroll," snickered Rashka, roosting in his usual fashion. "Have you brought me the pebbles you promised?"

Petrushka handed him the bag without saying a word. Rashka emptied it into his big right hand and began counting with his left.

"Ninety-one, ninety-two, ninety-three. . . . There are ninety-three pebbles, and not one hundred," he said finally, looking at Petrushka out of the corner of his eye. "The knot will not be untied."

"But I collected a hundred pebbles in the mountains, and I counted them just now when I got home!" exclaimed Petrushka, falling on his knees and holding his arms out to Rashka. "Maybe some pebbles fell out between my house and here."

The demon looked at the bag and said, "You're right, there's a little hole. Go find me the missing pebbles."

But Petrushka raised his face to the sky and started to beat his chest, shouting "Saint Nikolai, crack the earth wide open if I didn't bring a hundred back with me! And now I don't even have the strength to stay on my feet."

"All right, brother, be quiet," said Rashka, backing off because the very mention of the saint sent shivers down his ugly spine. "I'll undo the knot and go look for my own stones!"

The demon tapped the rails and they untied easily. Then while Petrushka shouted and screamed the names of all the saints in heaven, Rashka scrambled back along the tracks toward the house. He kept his big hairy ears folded shut so as not to hear Petrushka's screams, which made him sick to his stomach.

He found the first pebble and then another, right in the middle of the tracks.

He had just spotted a third when he was run over from behind by the eastbound train and smashed into a thousand pieces — demons that drink tea and wear necklaces are mortal, you know.

Petrushka stopped shouting and stood up. He was so beat that he could have slept three days and eaten twenty bowls of cabbage soup. But as he approached his house he managed to dance a little jig and croak a happy song.